A DON BLUTH FILM

All Dogs Go To Heaven ™

CHARLIE'S FRIENDS

Based on the motion picture from
Goldcrest and Sullivan Bluth Studio Ireland Ltd.

Executive Producers
GEORGE A. WALKER and MORRIS F. SULLIVAN
Produced by
DON BLUTH ★ GARY GOLDMAN ★ JOHN POMEROY
Screenplay by
DAVID WEISS
Directed by
DON BLUTH
Storybook adapted by
ANDREA KAMINSKY
Illustrated by
MILT NEIL PRODUCTIONS

Watermill Press
Mahwah, New Jersey

Charlie, a dog that is part shepherd and part scoundrel, is escaping from the pound with the help of his pal Itchy. Itchy, a friendly dachshund, is busy drilling as Charlie warns, "Careful Itchy. I think that might be a water main."

The warning is too late. A tower of water streams out from the pipe and the two make their getaway through a flood of water. The sounds of sirens fill the night.

They reach the floating nightclub, "Carface and Charlie's Place." Charlie's name has been crossed out from the sign in front.

Inside the boat, dogs watch rats running after cheese on a wild roller coaster track.

The customers are surprised when Charlie and Itchy make their entrance into the club. One of the regulars moans, "Things have changed, Charlie, since you've been gone."

"Carface hasn't been treating us too well," explains a small mutt.

The spotlight is on Charlie and Itchy singing "You can't keep a good dog down."

The place is jumping with happy hounds.

Carface's henchdog Killer can't believe his eyes when he sees Charlie. It was the greedy Carface and Killer who had arranged to have Charlie put away in the pound in the first place.

"I do not wish to share 50% of the business with my partner Charlie," Carface reminds Killer in his gravelly voice.

Charlie checks in with his old partner, Carface. Carface convinces him they can no longer be partners.

Carface throws a grand party to trick Charlie. A trusting Charlie is blindfolded and put at the end of a pier to wait for the "big surprise"— a surprise Carface has planned. A car is headed right for Charlie! Itchy's frantic calls to warn Charlie are too late.

"Where am I?" wonders Charlie. An elegant whippet explains that Charlie is on his way to heaven. Charlie insists a mistake has been made. But the watch that measures his life has stopped ticking.

Charlie charms the whippet, and rewinds his heavenly watch.

As he returns to Earth, he hears the haunting voice of the whippet, "You can never come back."

A coughing, gasping, water-logged Charlie makes his way back to Itchy.
A terrified Itchy screams, "Charlie . . . you're a ghost!"
"Do ghosts have fleas?" Once Charlie convinces Itchy that he is alive,
Itchy tells Charlie that Carface has a monster in his basement.

Charlie and Itchy spy on the monster in Carface's basement. The "monster" is a lovable orphan named Anne Marie. She can talk to animals! Charlie sees his chance to strike it rich. He promises Anne Marie a better life and takes her to his home.

Charlie tells Anne Marie a bedtime story. Anne Marie begins her prayers. When she asks God to bless Charlie, he is stunned. His heart melts when he hears her gently say, "And please help me find a mommy and daddy."

The next day, Charlie, Itchy and Anne Marie pay a visit to the stable so the little girl can find out from the horses which horse will win a race.

She will only do this if Charlie promises to give the money to the poor and help her find a mommy and daddy.

"I promise," Charlie agrees.

A big horse whispers to Anne Marie that the Grand Chawhee will win because it is his birthday.

Anne Marie finds a couple that she would like for her Mommy and Daddy. But Charlie takes the man's wallet to pay for their adventure. Then the Grand Chawhee comes in first! And so begins their winning streak.

Anne Marie gets new dresses and they build a new club. After much planning and work, it is time for the grand opening of Charlie's Place!

"Charlie's alive and I know he's got the girl," Carface growls. Carface makes plans to get rid of Charlie and get Anne Marie back.

Anne Marie insists that Charlie keep his promise to share the money with the poor. They go to an abandoned church to deliver pizza to a dog named Flo and to some orphan puppies.

"Charlie!" the delighted puppies greet their pal.

While Charlie is leading the puppies in a song and dance, Anne Marie finds the wallet from the couple at the stable. Anne Marie is disappointed in Charlie.

Up in the attic, she daydreams about what life would be like with the family in the photo from the wallet. She decides to return the wallet to them.

The next day Anne Marie goes to the "Wallet" family and enjoys a delicious breakfast with them. Charlie follows and wins back the kind-hearted Anne Marie. But Carface is out to get them!

Anne Marie and Charlie escape into a warehouse and fall into an underground swamp below.

"Charlie, what's that moving in the water?" Anne Marie asks, as a huge hungry alligator surfaces.

King Gator crows, "Ah, you look tasty!" The gator pops Charlie into his mouth. Charlie howls one of his famous yodels. King Gator takes Charlie out of his mouth and asks, "Oh, what do you call that voice, little fella? A baritone or a tenor?"

The two are instantly pals and sing a bouncy duet. But now Anne Marie has a terrible cold.

A worried Charlie takes a very sick Anne Marie back to Flo.

"You're not my friend," Anne Marie sobs. "You're a bad dog." Anne Marie thinks Charlie is only pretending to be her friend. She runs out coughing and crying into the rain.

Of course, Charlie really loves Anne Marie and chases after her.

Charlie hears Anne Marie's scream. Carface has captured her!
Itchy spreads the word, "Charlie's in trouble and a little girl may die."
Charlie has to fight Carface and his thugs, but there are too many of
them. Charlie howls his fabulous yodel. King Gator hears and comes
to help.

Charlie's love for Anne Marie is put to the test. He must choose between his life and the drowning Anne Marie. Charlie saves Anne Marie.

Later that night, Anne Marie and Itchy are safely tucked into bed at the "Wallet's" home.

Since Charlie has given his life for Anne Marie, the beautiful whippet from heaven calls gently, "Charlie, you can come back now." It is time for Charlie to say goodbye to Anne Marie.

Anne Marie is glad to see Charlie. "Oh Charlie, I'll miss you," Anne Marie sighs as she hugs and kisses Charlie. "I love you."

"I love you too," Charlie admits.

And then Charlie is gone in the glowing light.